Introduction

This book explores the beautiful complexity of love and fate, revealing that sometimes, things fall into place not because they're meant to be perfect, but because they are meant to be real. Fate doesn't bring us together for no reason—it nudges us toward one another when we need it most, even when we're least prepared for it. This story captures that moment when the universe conspires in inexplicable, yet necessary ways, offering us a glimpse into the transformative power of love.

I hope this story touches your heart
in the quietest, deepest ways —
and stays with you, long after the
last page.

Let the pages wrap around you :)

The Return

I stared out of the car window, watching the streets of India unfold before me like a scene from a distant memory. The chaotic hum of the city—the honking cars, the chatter of pedestrians, the bright colors of the street markets—felt both familiar and foreign all at once. It had been seven years since I last set foot here.

Seven long years.

The India I had left behind was a different world from the one I had returned to. Back then, everything seemed so simple. The scents of

spices in the air, the bustling
markets, the warm, welcoming
chaos of it all. It was home. But
now, after years of living abroad,
those same things felt like they
were smothering me. I felt like a
stranger, an outsider in my land.

 My mother had greeted me at the
airport with tearful eyes and a tight
embrace, the kind of embrace that
tried to make up for lost time. The
type of embrace that said, "I've
missed you so much, but I don't
know how to make you feel like
you're truly home again." I shifted
uncomfortably in my seat, trying to
ignore the dissonance building
inside me. The world outside was
moving at its usual pace, but I was

stuck—caught in a place where nothing seemed to fit. Not my life, not my family, and not myself.

After seven years in a foreign country, I had become accustomed to a life that was fast-paced, independent, and free of the expectations that had defined my childhood. I had built a career, made friends who didn't judge my every move, and developed a rhythm that felt… right. But here, in the sprawling lanes of my old neighborhood, it was as though the ground beneath my feet was constantly shifting.

My mother's home had barely changed. The same floral curtains hung by the window, the same brass statue of Lord Ganesha stood on the mantle. The scent of fresh jasmine still lingered in the air, just like it had when she was a child. But everything felt like it was from another lifetime—a life she no longer recognized.

"You'll get used to it," my mother had reassured me earlier that morning as we sat together at the breakfast table, the only sound the clinking of teacups. "You'll see, it's not the same as before. You'll find your place again." But I wasn't so sure. How could I fit into a world that had moved on without me?

My cousins, with whom I had
once spent endless summers, had
changed. Their lives were now
filled with children, obligations,
and routines that made me feel like
I had stepped into someone else's
life. They treated me like a guest,
and every glance held a question:

Who are you now? My childhood
friends, those I had been so close
to, were now distant and polite.
They had built lives around the
expectations of society, marriages,
careers, and children—things I
wasn't sure I wanted to embrace
just yet.

The old me, the one who had run
around these streets with carefree

abandon, was no longer here. The girl who had dreamed of leaving India to carve out her destiny now stood in the shadow of expectations and the weight of family pride.

And then there was society—the ever-watchful, judgmental eyes of the world I had hoped I could escape. There were whispers, subtle but undeniable, about my life choices. About my "westernized" way of thinking, my refusal to conform, my inability to fit into the neatly defined roles that society seemed to have for women like me. I had always known I was different. But now, I felt it more than ever. Sitting in my room that

evening, staring out at the bustling
street, I couldn't help but wonder if
coming back was a mistake. Was
this the life I was meant to return
to? Or was I just the product of my
faded memories?

"Ilahi," my mother's voice called
from downstairs, breaking my train
of thought. "Dinner's ready."
With a deep breath, I pushed
myself off the windowsill,
smoothing the wrinkles in my
dress. I made my way downstairs,
trying to push away the feeling of
not quite fitting in, of not quite
belonging. As I sat at the dinner
table, surrounded by family
members who were eager to catch
up, my thoughts kept drifting back

to one question: Is this really
where fate wanted me to be?
 Perhaps in time, I would learn to
understand the forces that had
brought me here. But for now, it
was a struggle—a struggle to find
my place, to reconcile the Ilahi
who had left and the one who had
returned.

 Maybe, just maybe, the girl in the
mirror was still trying to find out
who I was and where I truly
belonged.

The Weight of Judgment

 The weekend after my return was
a whirlwind of family gatherings,
loud conversations, and forced
smiles. It was the kind of event I
had once been a part of, back when
I had lived here, but now it felt like
a stage I was forced to perform on,
a role I didn't recognize.
 My mother had insisted I attend
despite my frailty.
"You should reconnect with
everyone, beta," my mother said,
though her voice was soft with
exhaustion. "Family is everything.
You'll see, it'll be good for you."
 I didn't have the heart to argue. I
knew my mother was trying to

hold onto what little was left of her
strength. So, I went— dressed in
the traditional sari my mother had
insisted I wear— smiling and
nodding at relatives I hadn't seen
in years. But as soon as I stepped
into the large family gathering, the
heavy weight of judgment hit me
like a wave. My aunt, Nancy, had
been the first to speak, her eyes
narrowing as she took in my
presence. "So, Ilahi," she had said,
her voice dripping with polite
curiosity.
"You've come back after all these
years. What made you decide to
leave your life in London? It's not
easy to leave everything behind,
especially for your mother, right?"

The question hung in the air, thick with unspoken criticism. It wasn't the kind of inquiry you asked someone you genuinely cared about. It was a judgment—a judgment wrapped in concern but with a sharp edge.

I had forced a smile, resisting the urge to snap back. I knew exactly where this conversation was going. The relatives had already begun whispering behind my back. The ones who hadn't seen me in years saw my return as nothing more than a backward step, a failure of sorts. After all, a young woman with a career in the West shouldn't just abandon it to take care of her ailing mother, should she?

"Family is important," I said, her voice steady, though I felt my heart sink. "I'm here because my mother needs me. That's all."
 The silence that followed felt oppressive. A few of my cousins exchanged looks, and I could see the judgment in their eyes. Had she made the wrong choice? Was she making a mistake? As I moved deeper into the crowd, it didn't get any easier. The conversations around me seemed to mock my every decision. There was talk of success, marriage, children—everything I was supposed to have achieved by now, according to their standards. They spoke of the "perfect" life—working hard, marrying

young, building a family. They didn't understand my choice. They didn't understand the weight of the decision that had driven me here. "You know," another cousin said, this time, it was Riya—my older cousin who had always been the epitome of conventional success. "It's a brave thing you're doing, coming back for your mother. But have you thought about what this will mean for you? You can't just stay here forever. What about your career? What about your future?" The words hit harder than they should have. I tried to hold my ground, though inside, I felt the pang of doubt creeping in.
What about my career?
What about my future?

Was this really what I wanted?
 I glanced over at my mother,
sitting quietly in the corner,
surrounded by people who barely
seemed to notice her fragile
condition. My mother, Seema, had
always been the pillar of strength
in our family, the one who had
made countless sacrifices to give
me the life I had. Now, I knew that
my mother was fading. I had seen
the signs—the slow loss of energy,
the deepening wrinkles, the way
her hands trembled slightly when
she reached for a cup.
 My heart twisted with the
realization that my mother might
not have much time left. And no
matter what anyone else thought, I
knew this was where I was meant

to be. I wasn't here for judgment. I wasn't here to explain my decision. I was here because my mother needed me. And that was enough. Later that evening, as the crowd thinned out and the house grew quieter, I retreated to my mother's room. The only sounds were the soft rustling of the jasmine outside the window and the rhythmic ticking of the old clock on the wall. My mother looked up as I entered, giving her a tired smile.

"You look exhausted, beta."

I sat beside her, taking her frail hand in mine. "It's just… a lot," I admitted, my voice low. "Everyone has their opinions, Mom. They think I've made the wrong choice, coming back." My mother's gaze softened, and she squeezed my hand gently. "Let them talk, my dear.

 People will always have something to say. They don't know the full story, not the way you do. You're here for me, and that's all that matters." I took a deep breath, my chest heavy with the weight of it all. "I don't regret being here for you, Mom. I don't. But sometimes, it feels like everything I've worked for is slipping away."

 My mother gave me a knowing smile. "Life isn't always about what we've built for ourselves, Ilahi. Sometimes, it's about what we leave behind. You've built a beautiful life, but sometimes, we have to let go of one thing to hold on to another." I closed my eyes, trying to absorb my mother's words.

It was true—I had left behind my life, my independence, everything that had made me feel in control. But my mother's health was the priority now. I wasn't here because I had to be, but because I chose to be. And no amount of judgment from extended family or society would change that. That night, as I lay in bed, the doubts still lingered at the edge of my mind, but they no longer held the same power over me.

I knew that no matter what anyone else thought, I had made the right decision. My family—especially my mother—had always been there for me. Now, it was my turn to be there for them. In the quiet of my room, with the sound of the night outside and my mother's soft breathing just down the hall, I made a silent vow to myself: I would stand strong. No matter how hard it got, no matter how much the world judged me, I would stay. For my mother, for family, for the love that had always been unconditional.

Strain of Adjusting

 Three months. It had been three months since I had returned to India, and though I had slowly started to settle into a new rhythm, the reality of living here—of being home—felt like an endless cycle of adjustments.
 The sweltering heat of the Indian summer was relentless. Even in the early mornings, when the city was still sleepy, the humidity seemed to cling to my skin, making everything feel ten times harder. I had spent the first few weeks trying to convince myself that I could handle it, but the heat wasn't something I could ignore. It seeped

into my bones, making me tired
and sluggish.

 And then there was the food. After
years of living abroad, my body
wasn't used to the spices, the
heavy meals, the rich gravies, and
deep-fried snacks. The sudden
change in diet, coupled with the
heat, had begun to take a toll on
my health. The constant bloating,
fatigue, and stomach aches were a
constant reminder that I wasn't in
London anymore. It wasn't just the
food, either— I was eating at
irregular hours, trying to keep up
with the fastpaced family
gatherings and late-night
celebrations that were an intrinsic
part of life here.

But despite the physical
discomfort, I kept pushing through.
There was no room for weakness,
not when there was so much to do.
The festivals had come and gone in
a blur. First, it was Rakhi, a
celebration of siblings and familial
love. I had tied the traditional rakhi
on my elder brother's wrist, though
the gesture felt strange after so
many years apart. We had grown
up together, but time had changed
things. My brother was now more
mature with his own life, and I was
a woman with responsibilities she
hadn't had before. We exchanged
gifts, but the moment felt like a
quiet reminder of everything I had
missed, everything that had shifted
in the years I had been away. Then

came Ganesh Chaturthi, the
festival of Lord Ganesha, and I had
watched as the neighborhood came
alive with the sounds of drums and
chants. The idol was brought into
our home—carefully placed in the
center of the living room—while
the family prepared for the
festivities. The familiar smell of
incense filled the air, mingling with
the spices from the kitchen as my
aunts and cousins worked together,
preparing food for the traditional
feast. I joined in, feeling both a
part of something and yet apart
from it all. The laughter, the
singing, the rituals—it was all so
familiar, so comforting. But
something inside me tugged with
unease. I was still adjusting. My

body was still reeling from the constant changes. My mother, always the heart of the home, smiled at me with warmth, but I could see the fatigue in her eyes. She had tried her best to participate in the festival, to make sure everything was as it had been in years past, but her illness was a constant reminder of how fragile everything was.

 I had spent the last few months trying to balance being a caregiver with being a part of my family. I had thrown myself in to the celebrations, keeping myself busy, trying to push through the physical discomfort, but there were moments when the weight of everything—my mother's illness, my health struggles, and the pressure to fit back into a life I barely recognized—became too much.

 That evening, after the Ganesh Chaturthi festivities had wound down and the last of the guests had left, I retreated to my room, exhausted. The heat and the noise had drained me, but it wasn't just that. My stomach churned from the rich food, and I felt a persistent headache coming on. I had grown accustomed to the sensation by now—the physical toll that living here had taken on my body—but tonight, it felt worse than ever. I didn't know how much more I could take. "Maybe it's time for a change," I whispered to myself, sitting on the edge of the bed. I pulled my knees up to my chest and hugged them tightly. I had been so focused on my mother, on making sure everything at home was inorder,that I hadn't taken the time to care for myself. My health was deteriorating in subtle ways, and I knew it. The fatigue had become unbearable. The heat was taking its toll on my skin, my energy, and my focus.

 As much as I tried to embrace the life I had returned to, there were days when I felt like a stranger in my own body. I missed the cool, temperate weather of London, the consistent routines I had followed there, the food that hadn't been so hard on my digestive system. But

most of all, I missed the feeling of
being in control—of knowing what
to do next.

 I thought back to the conversation
I had with my mother just a few
days ago, when my mom had
quietly mentioned how much better
I seemed compared to when I first
arrived. But I knew better. I had
become adept at hiding the
exhaustion behind a smile, at
pretending everything was okay.
"I'm not okay," I muttered softly to
myself, the words hanging in the
air as if finally speaking them
would make them true. I reached
for my phone and typed a quick
message to my childhood friend,
Meera. She had always been a
listening ear, and even though we

hadn't spoken in months, I felt an odd comfort in knowing that someone, somewhere, could understand.

I miss you. I feel like I'm losing myself here. I don't know what to do anymore.

I stared at the screen, my thumb hovering over the "send" button. I hesitated, unsure if reaching out would make me feel better or worse. Finally, I. pressed send, then set the phone down, sinking back into the bed, closing my eyes against the overwhelming fatigue. I wanted to escape—to go back to the life I had worked so hard for, where I wasn't constantly battling my body's exhaustion and the unspoken judgments of society.

But deep down, I knew that wasn't possible. Not now. Not when my mother needed me. I had made a choice, and there was no going back. The sound of laughter from downstairs filtered up through the walls, reminding me of what I had left behind—and what I still had to face.

Unseen Storm

 Life had started to feel a little
easier, a little more manageable.
With each passing day, I adjusted
more to the heat, the food, the
crowded streets of Mumbai, and
most importantly, my mother's
care. I had learned to find small
pockets of peace amidst the chaos.
The festivals were over for now,
and while they had been draining,
they had also served to bring me
closer to the family I had once
known so well.
 My health was slowly improving,
too. I had made adjustments to my
diet, cut back on the heavy foods
that had been giving me stomach

trouble, and started drinking more water to keep myself hydrated under the relentless sun. But more than that, the social and emotional barriers were beginning to soften. I was starting to find myself fitting in—once again becoming part of the tapestry of family life I had left behind.

 I have begun to spend more time with my cousins, laughing and chatting like I had when I was younger. The familiarity of the conversations about childhood memories, about people we both knew, and the occasional gossip made me feel like I hadn't been away at all. I had even started meeting old friends—like Meera, who I would chat with on the phone when the loneliness became too overwhelming.

In some ways, it felt like things were finally starting to fall into place. I was adjusting to the rhythm of life here, and the constant tension that had once plagued me—of not belonging, of feeling like an outsider—was slowly fading away. But there was one storm I hadn't expected, one I wasn't prepared for: Marriage.

It started with my aunt, Ayesha, casually mentioning it during one of our lunch gatherings.

"You know, Ilahi," Ayesha had said, her voice low and almost conspiratorial. "You're at the perfect age. It's time for you to start thinking about settling down.

You've been back for a while now, and you're 24 already. You don't want to wait too long." I had almost choked on my water, quickly recovering with a nervous laugh. "Aunt, I'm not in any rush," I replied, trying to deflect the conversation. But my aunt wasn't letting it go. "Well, the right time is now, Beta. You've been away for so long, and now that you're here, you should make the most of it. I know a nice boy, a friend of your uncle's. He's been asking about you to introduce you to his son." My stomach tightened. I had heard these words so manytimes, back when I was living in London. But now that I was here, they felt like an insistent weight pushing down

on me, suffocating me in ways I
hadn't anticipated. My mother, too,
had started dropping hints.
"Maybe it's time for you to meet
someone, Ilahi. You know, settling
down could bring you peace. I
want to see you happy."
I felt a knot form in my chest.
Happiness. The kind of happiness
that came with love and marriage
felt so distant, so out of my reach. I
couldn't deny that the idea of
marriage terrified me.
I had been in love before, or at
least I had thought I was. I had
given my heart to people who
didn't deserve it, and each time, I
had been left broken. The scars
from those failed relationships
were still there, hidden beneath the

surface, but they were deep, and they ran through my heart like invisible threads of pain.

The first time I had truly fallen in love,it had felt like magic. He had been my best friend, someone I could confide in, someone who had made me feel like I wasn't alone in the world. But in the end,he had walked away, leaving me devastated and questioning everything I had believed about love.

The second time had been more painful. He was everything my family had wanted for me—successful, well-spoken, and from a good family—but he hadn't been the right person for me. I had invested so much into the relationship, hoping that if I just tried harder, it would work. But in the end, his commitment to the relationship had been lukewarm, and my own heart had been left shattered once again. By the time I left for London, I had been so afraid of love that I had shut myself off completely. I had convinced myself that love wasn't worth the risk, that it would only hurt me again. I had focused on my career, my independence, everything I could do to avoid that vulnerability.

But now, sitting here in India, surrounded by well-meaning relatives and family, the pressure to marry was mounting. Every conversation seemed to circle back to the topic—how I was "getting older" and how it was time for me to think about my future, about "settling down."

 The more they spoke about it, the more I recoiled. The idea of marrying someone I barely knew felt like a trap. I wasn't ready to let anyone in. I wasn't ready to risk my heart again. That evening, after a particularly long day of running errands for my mother, I found myself alone in my childhood bedroom, staring at the photo of my younger self on the dresser. I had been so carefree back then. Now, at 24, everything seemed so heavy. I closed my eyes,leaning my head back against the wall, letting the cool air of the fan wash over me. I wasn't ready for marriage. I wasn't ready to open my heart to someone, not when I was still recovering from the wounds of my past. But how could I convince my family of that? They didn't understand. They only saw me as a young woman who was running out of time, someone they needed to marry off before it was too late. "Maybe I'm just being selfish," I whispered to myself, though I didn't believe it. I wasn't asking for the world, just the space to figure out my own life on my terms.

 I stood up, pacing the room, frustration and fear welling up inside me. I needed to talk to my mother, but every time I tried, the

words caught in my throat. How
could I explain to her that, despite
everything, despite the love I had
for her, I wasn't ready to take that
step? I couldn't bear to disappoint
her again, not after everything I
had done to care for her.
 But how could I move forward if I
wasn't being true to myself?

The Meeting that Felt Empty

For days, I had tried to avoid it,
convincing myself that I wasn't
ready. But my parents had been
persistent—more persistent than I
would ever have seen them. After
weeks of nudges and subtle hints,
my mother and father had finally
convinced me to take the first step.
"Just meet him, beta. You don't
have to make a decision right
away," my mother had pleaded.
"Just see for yourself."
They had found his profile on a
matrimonial site, just like they had
done with countless others. A
well-educated, decent man from a

good family, a solid match by all standards. But I wasn't convinced. I wasn't looking for a match. I wasn't looking for a "good family." I was looking for someone who could make me feel like my heart wasn't broken, someone who could make me feel alive again. And that… that was something I feared might never come.

 But in the end, the pressure had gotten to me. I didn't want to disappoint my parents. I didn't want to feel like I was shutting myself off from a possibility that everyone else seemed to think was right for me. So, with a deep breath and a heart full of doubts, I agreed to meet him. The day of the meeting came, and I found myself standing in front of the mirror, adjusting my white Indian suit. The soft fabric of the suit draped elegantly over my frame, and I could already see the slight glow in my skin. For a moment, I could almost forget how nervous I was, how every inch of my body was screaming that this wasn't right. My mother had insisted on the bindi—"It looks beautiful, beta. You'll look so graceful." I tried to appreciate the sentiment, but it felt like another expectation I wasn't sure I could meet.

I had always prided myself on being independent, on not needing anyone to complete me. But now, standing there in front of the mirror, I couldn't help but feel vulnerable.

What if I didn't like him?

What if this was just another one of those forced encounters that made me feel more alone than ever?

But I couldn't back out now. Not when my parents were so hopeful. "Everything will work out," they had said. I just had to give it a chance. The meeting was arranged at a quiet café in the city, a place chosen by his family to keep things formal and neutral. I arrived early, my palms slightly sweaty, my heart beating faster than usual. I sat at a corner table, nervously checking my phone, waiting for the time to pass. When his family arrived, they were polite and friendly, with smiles that didn't quite reach their eyes. His mother and father were warm enough, engaging me in small talk about my upbringing, my family, and the things I had been doing since I moved back to India. It was all very familiar—these were the conversations I had been hearing my whole life. But each word felt hollow, each gesture, though kind, felt like it was part of a script I couldn't seem to follow. And then, he walked in. He was tall, with neatly combed hair and an easy smile. He greeted me with a handshake,a polite but not overly enthusiastic one. I could feel his gaze lingering on me, but there was something about the way he looked at me—almost as if he were scanning me like a list of requirements, checking off boxes. He sat across from me, and the conversation began. We spoke about our careers, our families, our education. It was all so… surface-level. So practiced. I could tell that he was trying to make an impression, just as I was, but neither of us seemed able to break past the pleasantries. We exchanged numbers after the meeting—just as expected— and began chatting over text messages. At first, the conversations were cordial, polite exchanges of "How are you?" and "What are you doing?" But as the days wore on, I found myself unable to connect with him. No matter how hard I tried, it all felt so forced. I would message him, trying to keep the conversation going, but my replies were mechanical, as if I were simply going through the motions. I didn't feel the spark I had once hoped to feel when I imagined meeting someone new. I didn't feel the excitement or the anticipation. All I felt was… numb. I would tell myself that maybe it was just the beginning, that things could change, but deep down, I knew that this wasn't what I wanted. I didn't want to spend my life trying to make something work that didn't come naturally. I wasn't ready to settle for a life that felt forced, that felt like an

arrangement. One night, after
another mundane conversation
with him, I set my phone down on
the table. I had tried, but it was
clear now that there was no
emotional connection. No
chemistry. I wasn't sure what I had
expected, but it certainly wasn't
this. A sense of emptiness washed
over me. I had done what my
parents had wanted. I had given it a
chance. But now, I was more
certain than ever that this wasn't
the path I wanted to walk. I wasn't
ready for a relationship like
this—not one where I had to keep
convincing myself it would work. I
sighed, staring at my reflection in
the window. The world outside
seemed to blur as I fought to

swallow the disappointment that had begun to settle deep inside me. This wasn't just about him. It was about me. About the walls I had built around my heart, the fear that had taken root inside me and made it impossible to let anyone in.

 I wasn't ready for marriage. Not now. Not with him. Not until I could figure out what I truly needed, what I truly wanted. But how could I explain that to my parents? How could I tell them that I wasn't ready to take such a monumental step, that I wasn't ready to settle for a life that didn't feel like mine?

The Search For Something Real

 My life had become a constant
cycle of meetings, expectations,
and disappointments. My
parents—well-established and
wealthy in their own right—had set
high standards for the man they
wanted for me. They weren't just
concerned about his family
background, his education, or his
career. No, it was much more than
that. They wanted someone who
could not only match their status
but also complement the image
they had carefully crafted for

themselves. Someone who could fit into their world, a world that wasn't just about love but about prestige and societal approval.

I had never cared about money or status. I've always believed that money isn't everything. When it comes to finding a partner, there are so many deeper qualities to consider—things that go beyond material wealth. I understand that my parents only want what's best for me, that they want me to have all the resources necessary for survival and success in life. But when it comes to money, my outlook is different. It's not the foundation of my happiness or the measure of a meaningful connection. I had grown up in a

family that valued success, but I
had always believed that love, real
love, should come from
understanding, trust, and a shared
connection. But no one seemed to
see things my way. The pressure
was unrelenting. Even though I had
tried to meet people on my terms,
even though I wanted to find
someone who could make my heart
feel something, my parents'
expectations weighed heavily on
my choices. Every time I
considered dating someone myself,
I couldn't help but feel as if there
were a checklist running in my
mind—a list of requirements I
couldn't shake off. Would he be
from a respectable family? Was his
career stable? Was he

well-educated? And, above all, did he have the same social standing as my family? It didn't help that every time I met someone my parents introduced, it felt like I was going through the motions. The conversations were polite, sometimes engaging, but nothing ever clicked. I went through two more meetings, each one leaving me more drained and disheartened than the last. The first guy had been charming, good-looking, with a wellestablished career in finance. He had checked all the boxes, but the chemistry was missing. He spoke to me like I was a business transaction, calculating every word, weighing every gesture. It felt cold. The second guy had been

kind enough, but there was
something about his quietness that
unsettled me. It was as if he didn't
want to get to know me, as if the
whole meeting was just a
formality, a step toward getting
what he needed—an arranged
marriage that would seal both
families' futures.

After the third meeting, I had
given up hope. I had tried so hard
to convince myself that something
would work out, that I would find
someone who would make me feel
more than just "settling" for the
sake of family expectations. But
the spark, the connection, was
never there.

Days passed in a blur, and my
spirits sank lower with each failed

attempt. I had tried to push aside
the hope that I could find someone
who truly resonated with me. I had
accepted that this was my
fate—that my family's plan for me
was the only path forward.

Behind Unheard Sayings

 Ever since I was born, my parents
have been my foundation, my
unwavering support. They've
always let me live my life the way
I wanted—allowing me the
freedom to explore, to make
mistakes, and to grow at my own
pace. I never doubted that their
love for me was unconditional, and
in return, I respected their
guidance. But ever since I moved
back in, something had shifted. It's
like the rules had changed, and I

wasn't even given a chance to adjust.

 The freedom I once had seems to have evaporated. I used to go out when I wanted, meet friends, take spontaneous trips, and just live without having to account for every minute of my day. Now, I feel like a prisoner in my own home. There are constant restrictions. I'm not allowed to go out much, and when I do, there's always an unspoken list of places I can't go, people I can't see, and things I can't do. It's suffocating. The worst part is the shift in their stance on my marriage. I never imagined that our relationship would change so drastically. My parents have always been

open-minded, supportive of my
choices, and encouraging when it
came to my dreams.
 But now?
 It's like they don't even hear me
when I tell them I don't care about
the things they care about most.
They've become fixated on money,
status, and appearances, as though
love is just an afterthought, an
unnecessary complication in a
perfectly structured world.
 They talk to me like I'm naive like
my thoughts on love are childish
and unrealistic. They don't
understand that love isn't a
business deal. It's not about
calculating what you gain, what
you lose, and how you present
yourself to the world. Love is

about connection, trust, mutual respect, and shared moments. I don't care about the financial standing of the person I marry. I don't care if their family has a history of success. What matters is that they see me, the real me and that I can do the same for them.
 But they don't get it. They think I'm being rebellious or ungrateful, but what they don't realize is that I just want them to listen. I want them to hear me, to see that I need something different, something more than just another "deal" that fits into their perfect picture of how life should be. I've tried to explain myself, but every conversation feels like I'm hitting a brick wall. They don't see the

person I've become, the person
who needs space, independence,
and the freedom to make her own
decisions. I'm not a child anymore.
I deserve love, the kind that's real
and genuine. I deserve to have a
say in my own future, not one
that's dictated by their vision of
what's best for me.

 I don't know how much longer I
can handle this. Their expectations,
their need to control every aspect
of my life, it's too much. I'm
drowning in their love, but it's the
kind that smothers me rather than
sets me free. I need a breath, a
space to think, to feel, to make my
own choices. And maybe, just
maybe, I need them to understand

that love is more than just a
checklist of societal approval. It's
about being seen for who you truly
are.
 I deserve that. I deserve to be
understood.

Echoes of Lost Understanding

When I was young, I never got to
know my grandparents. They were
long gone before I was born,
leaving a gap in my life that I often
felt the weight of. But there was
one person who filled that space in
my heart: my great-grandfather. He
was the one who cared for me
when I needed it most, the one who
had a quiet way of understanding
me. Even when the world seemed
too loud, too complicated, he was
my refuge. He never judged me.
He didn't have the expectations my
parents had, or the pressure to

make me fit into some preordained mold. He simply saw me. Sometimes, I wonder if things would have been different if he were still alive. Maybe he would have been the one to understand me in ways no one else ever could. His wisdom, his calm demeanor, the way he would listen and let me talk without rushing to fix things—those are things I miss now more than ever. Maybe, just maybe, he would have helped me find a way to bridge the gap between my own dreams and my parents' expectations. He would have known that I wasn't being difficult, that I wasn't just rebelling—I was trying to find my own path, my own truth. I wish he

were here now, to help me navigate
this maze of confusion and doubt.
 I have my brother, of course. He's
a good person, kindhearted, and
well-meaning. But there's a
distance between us that I can't
quite bridge. He's so much like our
parents—he sees things the way
they do, values the same things
they do. His perspective is clouded
by the same ideals that have
suffocated me. I love him, but it's
hard to talk to him about this,
because I know he won't
understand. He won't see the world
through my eyes, the way my
great-grandfather once did. He
won't see the confusion, the
frustration, the yearning for
something real and genuine.

Right now, I feel more alone than
ever. Everyone around me is telling
me what I should do, how I should
live, who I should marry. But none
of that is what I want. None of it is
what I dreamed of. I didn't ask for
this life of expectations and
pressure. I didn't ask for the
checklist of qualities that I'm
supposed to find in someone else. I
just wanted someone who would
look at me the way I want to look
at them: with understanding, with
care, with the freedom to be
exactly who we are.

But here I am, caught in the space
between what I'm expected to want
and what I truly desire. I don't
know how to break free from this. I

feel like I'm screaming into the
void, but no one hears me. It's a
heavy, lonely feeling—knowing
that the people closest to you don't
see you the way you need to be
seen. And sometimes, I wonder if
it's even possible to find a way out
of this.
 I just want someone to understand
me. Not for what I could be, or
what they think I should be, but for
who I really am.

The Unexpected Connection

I don't really know what made me
do it. Maybe it was the loneliness,
the overwhelming sense of
isolation that had been building up
for weeks. Maybe I was looking
for someone to talk to, someone
who could listen without judgment,
without all the expectations that
seemed to follow me everywhere
else. Whatever the reason, I found
myself downloading a dating app
one night, my fingers hovering
over the screen as I debated
whether or not I should actually

take the plunge. I had always been
skeptical of the whole idea—of
meeting people through a screen,
reducing human connection to a
few carefully chosen pictures and
words. But in that moment, I
couldn't help but feel desperate. I
was tired of carrying everything
inside, of bottling up my feelings
in a place where no one could see
them.
Maybe this would be the answer.
Maybe, just maybe, I would find
someone who could understand
me, who could see beyond the
surface and into the person I truly
was. So, I created a
profile—halfheartedly, honestly,
unsure of what to expect. I didn't
fill out all the boxes with the usual

"looking for a relationship" or
"seeking fun and adventure" lines.
I couldn't bring myself to lie. What
was I really looking for? Someone
to share the quiet moments with,
someone who didn't expect
perfection, who wouldn't judge me
for not fitting into the mold my
parents and society had laid out for
me. I swiped through profiles, each
one more disconnected than the
last. It felt like I was searching for
something that didn't exist, or at
least something that wasn't meant
for me. Every time I swiped left, I
couldn't help but feel a little more
hopeless. Maybe I was chasing an
illusion, something I couldn't
define, or maybe I just didn't know
what I truly wanted anymore. But

then, I matched with someone. His
name was Kabir. My heart skipped
a beat. His photo immediately
caught my eye—dark hair tousled
perfectly, brown eyes that seemed
to hold secrets, and a slight smile
that made me wonder what was
behind it. He looked like someone
I could get lost in, someone whose
presence would fill a room even
without saying a word. And I
couldn't stop looking at him. Every
time I saw his photo, my heart did
a little flip. I stared at his profile
for what felt like an eternity.
Something about his calm yet
intense expression drew me in, and
I couldn't shake the feeling that
there was more to him than just a
face in a picture. The way he held

himself, the quiet confidence in his eyes—it was magnetic. For a moment, I hesitated. I had been disappointed too many times already. What was the point? But, against my better judgment, I felt a spark of excitement. It was silly to think that one profile could change anything, but I was too curious to ignore it. After gathering my thoughts, I finally mustered the courage to send him a message. "Hey." To my surprise, he responded almost immediately. "Hey! How's it going?" That simple greeting was the start of something I hadn't expected. The conversation flowed easily—at first, it was small talk, the kind of conversation you have when you don't know where to start. We talked about the weather, about music, about nothing that really mattered. But with every passing message, I felt a connection building between us. There was something different about Kabir. He made me laugh effortlessly, and the way he responded to me was genuine. He seemed to care about everything I said, no matter how trivial it seemed. For the first time in weeks, I felt like I was talking to someone who wasn't trying to fit into some preconceived mold. He wasn't forcing anything. It was just… easy.

And then, out of nowhere, he called. It was 2 a.m. I froze, staring

at the screen. Who calls at 2 a.m.
on a dating app?
I almost didn't pick up. What was
this—was he for real?
But something about the tone of
his message made me pause. I
couldn't explain why, but I was
drawn to him in a way I hadn't
been with anyone else in a long
time. So, against my better
judgment, I answered. "Hey," he
said, his voice deep and soothing,
like a melody I never knew I
needed.
"I hope I'm not waking you up."
 I smiled despite myself, my heart
pounding in my chest.
"No, you're good. I just didn't
expect a call."

"Yeah, I figured. But I couldn't
sleep. I wanted to hear more of
your voice."
My breath caught in my throat. His
words were so sincere, so gentle,
that any remaining hesitation I had
melted away. It was as if he wasn't
just calling to fill the silence but to
connect. And that feeling, that
genuine desire to connect, was
enough to make me feel safe. We
continued talking, hour after hour,
as if time didn't matter. It was as if
we had known each other for much
longer than just a few days. The
conversation flowed effortlessly,
and with every word, I felt a little
more of the wall around my heart
come down. I wasn't sure what it
was about Kabir, but it felt

different from anything I had ever
experienced. At one point, I
realized how late it had gotten. I
stifled a yawn, but neither of us
was ready to end the call. "I should
probably let you get some sleep,"
he said, though his voice still
carried the warmth of someone
who didn't want to say goodbye. I
hesitated, but the thought of
hanging up felt like it would break
the fragile thread we had started
weaving between us.
"Yeah, I guess," I replied. But even
as I said it, I knew neither of us
was quite ready to say goodbye.
 We stayed on the phone for a little
while longer, just talking about the
most random things, from our
favorite childhood memories to the

small details of our everyday lives.
It felt natural. For the first time in a
long time, I felt like I wasn't
pretending to be someone I wasn't.
I wasn't hiding behind expectations
or obligations. I was just… myself.
And for that moment, it felt
enough.
 When we finally said goodnight,
both of us were left with the
strange feeling that we had just
scratched the surface of something
that could be far more than either
of us expected. I lay back in bed,
my mind racing with the echo of
his voice still lingering in my ears.
There was something about Kabir
that felt different.
 I wasn't sure if it was too soon to
say that I felt a connection, but it

was certainly the most real
connection I had experienced in
months—maybe even years.

A Voice in the Silence

 The more I talked to Kabir, the more I felt like I was finally able to breathe. For the first time in what felt like forever, I wasn't constantly measuring my every word, making sure I didn't step out of line. With him, it was easy—uncomplicated. I could share everything, from the smallest details of my day to the bigger, heavier things weighing on my heart. It was like I could finally be myself without having to justify every choice I made, without worrying about what others expected from me. He listened without judgment, always taking

everything I said in stride,
encouraging me to keep going, to
keep talking. But at the same time,
the pressure at home was only
growing. It had been a few weeks
since I'd started talking to Kabir,
and every day felt like a battle
between the comfort I found in our
conversations and the crushing
weight of my parents' relentless
pursuit of a "suitable match." They
didn't care that I was finally
finding someone who saw me for
who I really was, someone who
made me feel like I mattered. No,
every day brought a new profile,
another potential candidate they
thought I should consider. Another
guy whose family was respectable,
whose career was impressive,

whose background checked all the boxes they had drawn up for me. And the constant barrage of profiles never seemed to end. Each time they presented another candidate, I felt a piece of myself breaking off. It wasn't just about rejecting their idea of who I should marry; it was about feeling like I wasn't allowed to choose my own path, my own future. Every time they came to me with another name, another set of expectations, it was like they were telling me, "You don't matter. Your happiness doesn't matter. Only our vision of your life does." I could feel the cracks forming in my soul, the exhaustion setting in as I tried to juggle my own desires and the endless pressure from my parents. I couldn't escape it. Even when I was with Kabir, sharing my thoughts, my frustrations, and my fears, I couldn't completely forget that back home, my life was being controlled by decisions I had no say in. But Kabir—he was different. He didn't judge me for how I felt. He didn't dismiss my struggles as insignificant. When I talked about my parents, the constant pressure, the endless profiles, he didn't try to fix everything. Instead, he listened, truly listened, and offered support in a way I hadn't experienced before. It wasn't about trying to make me feel better with empty words or advice. It was about letting me express everything I was going through, without trying to change how I felt. "You don't have to carry all of this alone," he said one evening, after I had unloaded yet another frustration about my parents. "You deserve to have a say in your own life. Don't let anyone take that away from you."

His words hung in the air, resonating deeply. I hadn't realized just how much I needed to hear them. My whole life, I'd been shaped by the expectations of others, told what I should want, who I should be. But Kabir—he didn't see me through anyone else's lens. He saw me for who I really was.

For the first time, I felt a glimmer of hope. Maybe there was a way out of this, a way to take control of my own life, even if it meant stepping away from everything I had known. Maybe Kabir wasn't just someone to talk to. Maybe he was the person who could help me find the courage to break free from this suffocating cycle.

Against All Odds

Kabir's life was so different from mine, so far removed from the sheltered world I had grown up in. The more I learned about him, the more I found myself in awe. He wasn't like the men my parents had introduced me to, the ones who lived their lives following the paths laid out for them by family and society. Kabir had built everything he had on his own, brick by brick, with a determination and strength that most people couldn't even begin to understand. He was the kind of person who worked tirelessly, who never rested,always chasing after his dreams,but doing

it on his terms. He wasn't born into
wealth or privilege. He didn't have
a family legacy to rely on. What he
had was pure grit. He started
working at an early age, taking on
responsibilities that most people
his age wouldn't have been able to
handle. He learned the value of
hard work, sacrifice, and
perseverance long before most
people even knew what those
words meant. What broke my
heart, though, was how little his
family seemed to appreciate his
efforts. They saw him as just
another person in the family who
should have followed the
traditional path, married the right
person, and adhered to the same
expectations they held for

everyone else. No matter how
much he achieved, no matter how
far he came, it was never enough
for them. They never truly saw the
depth of his sacrifices, the
sleepless nights, the moments
when he could have given up but
chose not to. It made me sad,
seeing someone so extraordinary
being treated like just another cog
in a machine. Kabir wasn't
ordinary. He was exceptional. And
it hurt to know that the people who
should have been the most proud
of him were the ones who seemed
the least appreciative.
 But Kabir didn't let that stop him.
He didn't let his family's lack of
recognition dull his spirit. If
anything, it seemed to fuel him.

His belief in family, in love, in
spreading kindness to those he
cared about—those values were
what kept him going. Despite
everything, he still believed that
keeping the family together,
showing love to those who
mattered, was the most important
thing in life. He didn't let his
circumstances or the lack of
support from his family change the
way he saw the world.
 And that's what made him stand
out. That's what made him
extraordinary. He didn't need the
approval of others to keep going.
He didn't need anyone's validation
to know he was on the right path.
He had built his life from the
ground up, all on his own, and in

the process, he had become
someone who was capable of
achieving anything. There was a
quiet strength in him, a quiet belief
that no matter what life threw at
him, he could handle it. As I
listened to him talk about his
journey—his struggles, his
triumphs, the setbacks and the
victories—I couldn't help but feel
proud. Proud of him, proud of how
far he had come, and proud of the
person he had become despite
everything life had thrown his way.
It wasn't just his achievements that
made him remarkable. It was his
heart, his willingness to love and
care for others, even when the
world hadn't been kind to him.

I wished, sometimes, that I could be as strong as he was. To have that same resilience, that same drive to push forward even when things seemed impossible. I couldn't imagine living the life he had, constantly fighting for everything he had, and yet, through it all, he still maintained this incredible sense of compassion for others.

I couldn't help but think—if only his family could see him the way I did. If only they could appreciate him for the incredible person he was, for all that he had sacrificed to get to where he was. But, then again, maybe it wasn't about their approval. Maybe, just maybe, it was enough that he knew what he

had achieved. That he knew his
worth, even if they never truly saw
it. I was proud of him. I admired
him. And in a way, I envied him
for his ability to rise above it all.
 But deep down, I couldn't ignore
the doubts. Would we click the
same way in person?
 Could we make this work with the
pressures from my family?
Could love like ours survive all the
expectations that weighed on us?
 I didn't know. But I couldn't stop
myself from feeling that pull. From
the beginning, it was like we were
destined to meet. It wasn't just
random, not just coincidence.
There was something more to it.
Something bigger. As I stood there,
staring at my phone, I realized that

no matter how scared I was, I was
ready for this. I was ready to meet
Kabir, to take that first step into
what could be a new chapter in my
life.
  We had already shared so much
without even meeting. But now, we
were finally going to see each
other face to face. As the
excitement surged within me, I
knew one thing for sure: no matter
where this journey led, it had
already been written in the stars.
Our meeting wasn't a coincidence.
It was fate.

The Moment of Truth

 As I sat there, staring at my phone screen, a sense of anticipation rushed through me. Kabir and I had spent so many hours talking, getting to know each other, and every conversation had felt like a step closer to something real, something I didn't expect to find. His voice, the way he made me laugh, the way he truly listened—it all felt so natural. It felt right. But despite everything feeling perfect, there was a nagging thought in the back of my mind. What if it all fell apart?

What if the moment we met, everything would come crashing down?

I couldn't shake the fear that my family wouldn't accept him. They had their minds set on a different kind of man—someone from a similar background, someone who fit their expectations of what was "proper." Kabir wasn't that person. He didn't have the business empire or the flashy life that my family valued so highly. And even though everything between us felt real, I couldn't ignore the fear that loomed over me—would my family ever accept him?

Would they see the things that I saw in him, the things that made me feel like he was the one?

I tried to push those worries aside.
After all, we hadn't even met in
person yet. This was all so new.
And yet, it felt like fate had
brought us together. Every
conversation, every shared laugh,
every time we confided in each
other—it felt like the universe had
been nudging us toward this
moment, toward finally meeting
face to face.
 When we decided to meet, it felt
like the right time. The months of
talking had built something
between us that neither of us could
ignore. It was more than just
physical attraction; it was a
connection. And I couldn't deny
that I was excited to see him, to
meet him, to see if the magic we

had on the phone could translate into real life.

 I couldn't stop smiling thinking about it. We were finally going to meet.My heart fluttered with excitement, and yet,at the same time, it felt like there was a weight on my chest.

What if it didn't go as well as I imagined?

What if we met in person and the connection wasn't the same?

What if my family never accepted him, and I had to choose between love and family?

But then I remembered what Kabir had told me once:

 "Sometimes, things are meant to be. Sometimes, universe brings two people together when they're

ready, even if they don't know it at
the time."
 I believed him. I believed that this
was destiny. Everything had led us
to this moment. I knew I had to
trust the process, trust the
connection we had, and let things
unfold as they were meant to. We
were both excited to meet, but in
different ways. Kabir was eager,
but there was an underlying calm
in his messages. He was confident
that we would be great together.
His faith in us made me feel a little
braver, a little more willing to take
the leap.

Dawn of Us

 The day had finally come—the
day I would meet Kabir in person.
I wanted to hear his heartbeat, to
feel the rhythm of it—how it
would mirror the way my chest
fluttered whenever I thought of
him. I imagined the sound, steady
and reassuring, filling the space
between us, making me feel like I
was exactly where I needed to be. I
wanted to be close enough to feel
safe, like we could face anything
together. I wanted to smell him, not
in some strange way, but in the
comforting, familiar way that told
me he was real. The scent would
wrap around me like a memory,

reminding me he wasn't just a
voice on the other side of a phone
or a picture in a profile. He'd smell
like home—the kind of home I
never realized I'd been searching
for. I could already feel the blush
creeping up my cheeks just
thinking about it. My pulse
quickened. The air felt charged,
like everything around me was
holding its breath, waiting for this
moment. It was as if the entire
world was in anticipation of us
meeting. The butterflies in my
stomach stirred with every passing
second, every inch closer to the
moment I would finally see him.
My body was electric, alive with
feelings I hadn't even known were
possible. The train clattered

beneath me, yet all I could hear
was the rapid pounding of my own
heart. Each passing station brought
me closer to him, and I couldn't sit
still. My hands trembled with
nervous anticipation. After all the
late-night conversations, the
laughter, the longing, the silent
dreams, we were finally about to
step into reality. My heart was
racing toward him before my feet
even hit the ground. When the train
finally slowed to a halt, the
moment stretched endlessly. I
stepped onto the platform, my eyes
scanning through the blur of
moving bodies. And then I saw
him. He stood there, tall, poised,
wearing a white and black shirt
that fit him too perfectly, like even

his clothes knew they were part of
my dream. For a second, I forgot
how to breathe. He looked exactly
how I had imagined, maybe even
more—his presence calm,
magnetic, and somehow already
familiar, like I'd known him
forever. We reached each other
through the crowd, and shared a
quick side hug—half awkward,
half beautiful. The platform was
too packed to stay still, but even
that fleeting touch sent warmth
through my whole body. In that
brief embrace, I could feel his
heartbeat against mine, steady and
real. We rushed out of the station
together, and the way he moved—
always slightly ahead of me,
looking back to make sure I wasn't

lost in the crowd—made me feel
wrapped in the gentlest protection.
He held the door of the cab open
for me like it was the most natural
thing in the world. I slipped in
beside him, our knees just barely
touching. My heart skipped a beat
again. He sat to my left, and for a
moment, he simply looked at me.
His gaze met mine, deep and
unblinking, and I felt like the world
hushed itself to make space for us.
Outside, traffic roared and people
shouted, but none of it reached me.
All I could hear was Kabir's
voice—low, warm, and a little shy
as he said my name for the first
time in person. The sound of it
wrapped around me like a secret. I
felt shy—so shy I could barely

hold his gaze—but there was a
smile tugging at my lips that just
wouldn't leave. It was the kind of
smile that only love can pull from
the soul, soft and endless. We
reached our stay for the night, and
after freshening up, we decided to
explore the area for dinner. The
streets were alive with colour and
light—restaurants glowing warmly,
laughter spilling from game
arcades, the soft hum of music
from nearby cafés. Everything felt
enchanted, like the city itself had
decided to play along with our love
story. We picked a cozy spot, and I
chose dosa for dinner. I could tell it
wasn't his favourite from the very
first bite, but he didn't
complain—not even once. He just

smiled and kept eating, his eyes
twinkling every time they met
mine. That simple act— eating
something just because I wanted
to—felt more intimate than words.
After dinner, we wandered toward
a claw machine at a small arcade
nearby. With playful determination,
Kabir gave it a go. I watched,
amused, as he concentrated like a
child on a mission. And
then—triumph. He picked a soft,
squishy teddy bear and handed it to
me with a proud little grin. I held it
close like it was a piece of this
night I could keep forever. When
we returned to our room, the
weight of the day settled into our
bones. We changed into something
comfortable, and as we lay on the

bed, it felt like time itself slowed down. Still buzzing from the night's joy, Kabir suddenly turned to me with a spark in his eyes, as if he'd just remembered something exciting. "Wait here," he said with a playful grin, disappearing for a moment. He returned holding two chilled bottles of something I'd never seen before. "It's called Mogu Mogu," he announced, his voice brimming with boyish excitement. "You have to try it." He looked like a kid showing off his favourite candy—eyes bright, hands eager, a little bounce in his step. He twisted the cap open for me and watched intently as I took the first sip, like my reaction was the most important thing in the

world. The sweetness, the chewy
texture, the unexpected delight of
it—it was all so refreshing, but
what stayed with me most was
him—the way he lit up just to
share something small with me. It
was such a simple moment, yet it
felt like everything. He pulled me
gently into his arms, and for the
first time, I felt completely still.
The noise, the world, the worries
of home— they all disappeared. In
his embrace, I felt like I belonged.
His warmth seeped into my skin,
anchoring me in a moment that
didn't need words. His hand
stroked my hair softly, and I tilted
my head toward him, meeting his
lips in a kiss that felt like a breath
held too long, finally released. It

wasn't rushed. It wasn't dramatic.
It was perfect—slow, reverent,
filled with every unsaid promise.
As we sat together, the quiet
wrapped around us like a soft
blanket. I suddenly remembered
one of our playful phone
conversations from a few nights
ago. He had told a little lie at work,
saying he was meeting a girl for
marriage. I had teased him in
return, joking, "You better not
come without a ring, mister." It
was meant to be silly, lighthearted,
just me messing around. But now,
in the stillness of the evening, I
turned to him and asked,
half-laughing,
 "So… did you actually bring a
ring?"

He smiled—but not the teasing
kind. There was something tender
and serious in his eyes.
"Close your eyes and count to ten,"
he said softly. My heart skipped.
"Wait, what?"
"Just trust me. Close your eyes."
So I did. I counted slowly,
nervously, my pulse racing with
every number.
 And when I opened my eyes…
There it was.
 A ring.
 A real ring.
 He was holding it gently, as if it
were more than metal and
stone—as if it were a promise.
Before I could even process what
was happening, he slipped it onto

my finger. I stared at it in stunned
silence—the most beautiful ring I
had ever seen, not just because of
how it looked, but because of what
it meant. He didn't need to say
anything. I could see everything in
his eyes—every late night, every
shared laugh, every moment of
waiting and longing. It all led to
this. In that instant, I just knew. I
had been right all along. This love,
this connection, this unshakable
bond between us—it was real. And
every bit of patience, every tear,
every lonely night we had endured
was worth it. All of it. He made
that moment unforgettable. Not
with grand gestures, but with
sincerity. With love. With
intention. And as I curled up beside

him, my fingers gently resting on
the ring he gave me, I felt the
rhythm of his heartbeat under my
cheek. The world fell away again,
leaving just the two of us—
tangled in warmth, in stillness, in a
kind of love I had only ever
dreamed of. This was real. This
was happening. And I couldn't
wait to wake up next to him—to a
new day, a new chapter, with his
arms still around me.
 Fate had brought us here. And as I
stood there in his presence, I knew
this was only the beginning of
what we were meant to be.

A Day to Remember

We woke up in each other's arms,
the same way we'd fallen
asleep—wrapped in warmth,
tangled in love. The morning
unfolded slowly, wrapped in
golden light and the soft rhythm of
our breath syncing in silence. I was
the first to stir, eyes fluttering open
to the stillness of the room and the
warmth of his body beside mine.
He looked peaceful, his face
softened by sleep, one arm still
draped protectively over me like
even in his dreams, he didn't want
to let go. I stayed there for a while,
quietly watching him, feeling that
familiar ache in my chest— the

kind that only comes when you're
completely, helplessly in love.
Every little detail about him felt
like home, and I found myself
falling all over again before the
day had even begun. I tried to
wake him up, gently at
first—running my fingers through
his hair, whispering his name. But
he refused to budge. I teased him,
poked him, even threatened to steal
the blanket, but he just groaned and
pulled me closer, burying his face
in my neck. "Five more minutes,"
he mumbled, voice thick with
sleep. And I laughed, because even
his laziness felt like love. He had
told me the night before that he
wanted to cook breakfast for me,
and I was genuinely excited. It

wasn't just about the food—it was
the way he planned it with so much
intention, like even the smallest
gestures were his love language.
As always, we started our day with
music. He played something
upbeat on the TV, setting the
perfect morning rhythm. He turned
to me with that familiar sparkle in
his eyes and said,
"Go shower and get ready, baby.
We've got a full day ahead."
I nodded, trying to hide the smile
stretching across my face, and
headed to freshen up while he
moved into the kitchen. The smell
hit me first—eggs, toast,
something warm and familiar—but
it tasted like magic. He'd made
eggs and bread with jam, a simple

meal, but it was honestly the most
delicious breakfast I'd ever had.
Maybe it was because he made it.
Maybe it was the way he looked at
me as I took my first bite, eagerly
waiting for my reaction like a kid
showing off his best drawing. He
didn't let me lift a finger. Not to set
the table, not to clean. He treated
me like royalty—like I was the
most important thing in his world.
And in that morning light, with
music playing, food on the table,
and love woven into every
moment… I realized I was falling
for him even deeper. Again and
again. We were all set to head out
for a cozy movie date and spend
some time wandering around the
mall. Getting ready together had

become its own kind of ritual—soft music in the background, shared mirrors, and stolen glances. Every single time, without fail, he'd look at me and say, "You look so pretty," with that soft sincerity that made my heart flutter. It didn't matter how many times he said it—it made me blush like it was the first. And then there was the ring. The one he gave me. I couldn't stop staring at it. Every five minutes, my eyes would drift down to my hand, tracing the shape of it like I still couldn't believe it was mine. It wasn't just a ring—it was a promise, a memory, a dream we were beginning to build.

Just when we thought we were all set, he accidentally put in the

wrong address for the movie
theatre. We both laughed when we
realized, but thankfully, we had
enough time to fix it. While
waiting for our cab, we found a
little café nearby and slipped inside
for a few moments of calm. We
ordered drinks and sat close,
clicking pictures and just holding
onto everything—the quiet, the
light in his eyes, the feeling of
being exactly where we were
meant to be. Every second felt like
a memory in the making, and I
didn't want to let a single one go
unnoticed. We finally reached the
mall, and he was practically
glowing with excitement for the
movie. His energy was
contagious—it made everything

feel even more special. We grabbed some fries and a couple of water bottles before heading into the theatre, all set and ready to escape into another world for a while. The movie was incredible—an action thriller woven with rich jazz music, exactly the kind of film he loved. I could see it in the way he leaned forward during certain scenes, his eyes lighting up with every twist. And all the while, our hands were intertwined— never letting go, like our own silent promise playing out beneath the sound of the screen. When the credits finally rolled and the lights came back on, we stood up to leave, still caught in that post-movie haze. And then, right at the exit, he noticed something—my shoelaces were untied. Before I could even react, he was already on his knees, fixing them for me with the most natural ease, like it was the most obvious thing in the world to do. People walked past us, glancing maybe, but he didn't care. Not even for a second. His focus was just on me—making sure I was okay, safe, cared for. It was such a small gesture, but it spoke volumes. I found myself falling even harder in that moment. He wasn't just the man I loved—he was the man who loved me back, out loud, without hesitation. After the movie, we roamed around the mall for a while, taking our time. There was no rush—just the joy of being

together. We wandered into a
bookstore, flipping through
random pages, pointing out titles to
each other, and letting the comfort
of quiet aisles and the scent of
paper wrap around us. We checked
out a few other stores too, laughing
at silly things, sharing small
moments that felt big in their way.
Soon enough, Kabir admitted he
was starving, and we decided to
head straight to the Italian café
we'd talked about earlier. The
place was beautiful—warm lights,
aesthetic decor, a cozy kind of
charm that made you want to stay
longer than planned. It was a little
crowded, filled with soft chatter
and the sound of kids playing
nearby. Somehow, that only added

to the warmth. We found our table and ordered my favourite—creamy risotto and a rustic-style pizza. The food looked almost too pretty to eat, but the real beauty was in the company. As we ate, we slipped into one of those long, heart-deep conversations. We started talking about kids—about our kids someday. How we'd raise them together, what kind of parents we wanted to be. His eyes lit up at the thought, and I could see him picturing that future as vividly as I was.

Somewhere between bites and smiles, we also joked about the things we'd do once we got back to the apartment. Then the conversation took a soft turn when

I mentioned how much he had
already spent on this trip. I knew
he just wanted to make everything
perfect for me, but I couldn't help
gently scolding him.
 "You need to start saving, love,"
I told him, half-serious,
half-teasing.
"You don't have to spend so much
to show me love—I already feel it
in everything you do."
 And he smiled, that boyish smile
that makes everything feel okay.
Because even in that crowded little
café, it was just us—and our dream
of a life we were slowly building,
one honest conversation at a time.
We finally reached the apartment,
and after such a long, tiring day, all
I wanted was to melt into the

comfort of his arms. The moment
the door closed behind us,the
outside world faded away. We
freshened up, changed into our
comfiest clothes, and curled up on
the bed, letting the silence settle
softly between us. We watched TV
for a while, not really
focused—just existing side by side,
our bodies close, hearts even
closer. Later, we decided to finish
the leftover ice cream from earlier,
so we took it out to the balcony.
The sky was dimming, the city
glowing beneath us, and the breeze
carried with it a kind of bittersweet
calm. It was the last night. The last
few hours. And no matter how
much I tried to hold on, time kept
slipping through my fingers. I

didn't want to leave. I didn't want
this to end. I just wanted to
stay—right there, with him,
forever. I've never felt more at
home than I do when I'm with him.
Not even my actual home gives me
this sense of peace. As we sat side
by side, sharing quiet spoonfuls of
ice cream and stolen glances, we
talked. About how hard it is—how
hard it's going to be. About our
families, our differences, the reality
we can't run from. We're not just
from different homes—we're from
different worlds. And still,
somehow, we found each other. I
told him the truth then— maybe
the hardest one-
"Even if one day you feel like
giving up, I won't. I'll fight for us,

even if I have to fight alone.
Because I love you.
And when I see my future… It's
you. It's always you."
In our heads, there's already a
house that belongs to us.
Where we argue over the perfect
spot for a couch.
Where we playfully fight for the
side of the bed with the charging
point.
Where we negotiate over who
cooks and who does the dishes or
decide to do it together.
Where we ask each other for just a
little more space in the cupboard.
Where he wraps his arms around
me from behind while I cook.
Where we steal spoonfuls of ice
cream straight from the tub.

Where we eat together, teasing
each other's feet under the table.
Where we curl up on the couch,
lost in a movie but more lost in
each other.
Where we fall asleep, tangled in
each other's arms.
 Where we leave for work together.
Where we fight and make up
within minutes.
Where we laugh and giggle on the
balcony, wrapped in a blanket,
looking at the moon.
A home that exists only in our
dreams.
For now.

The Hardest Goodbye

 It wasn't just the end of a trip.
Some goodbyes don't come with
words. They come with heavy
silences, stolen glances, and the
echo of a heartbeat you're trying so
hard not to forget. The morning
began like a slow unravelling. We
both knew what was coming. Still,
we laughed over breakfast, smiled
through our pain, pretending—just
for a moment—that we had more
time. That maybe if we moved
slowly enough, time would bend
for us. The night before, we made a
decision that would live with us
forever, and it was getting inked

together. The next morning, we
checked out and went straight to
the tattoo studio. The tattoo artist
almost refused; it was late, rushed,
and not ideal. But love doesn't
wait. It doesn't need perfect
timing. It just needs one moment of
undeniable truth, and we had that. I
kept asking him again and again,
"Are you sure?" because I know
what permanence really means. It's
not just about a design on
skin—it's about choice.
A choice to hold on.
A choice to remember.
And he was so sure. Surer than
I've ever seen him. And he didn't
even flinch. His eyes were calm.
Steady. Full of a kind of love that
doesn't just touch the body—it

wraps around the soul. I knew
then. I wasn't the only one
dreaming of forever. He was right
there with me. And finally, we got
inked—the number that held a
mark of everything we were,
everything we are, and everything
we hope to become. After that, we
went to lunch. It was warm food
and a cold ache in the heart. An
Indian restaurant nearby, soft
music in the background, clinking
cutlery, the kind of place that tried
to feel normal, but nothing felt
normal anymore. The goodbye was
coming. It was walking toward us
with every passing second, and we
had no shield against it. We barely
spoke, not because there was
nothing to say, but because no

words could soften what we were
about to face.

 Our goodbye.

 Our first real one.

 He was going back to his city. I
was going to a friend's. Two
different cabs. Two different roads.
But one shared heartbreak. We
waited outside for our rides. The
wind blew, light but cold, brushing
through the spaces between our
hands like it already knew it had to
separate us. I tried to act normal.
Smile. Joke. But inside, I was a
crumbling cathedral. Every minute
was a countdown I wasn't ready
for. We waited for the cab in
silence, but my heart was
screaming. Screaming to hold him
longer. To tell him I love him. To

ask him not to go. But I couldn't.
Not because I didn't feel it,
because I felt it too much. I was
scared that if I opened my mouth,
the pain would pour out like a
flood, and I wouldn't be able to
stop it. So I just stood there, beside
him, praying that my silence was
loud enough to say everything I
couldn't. When the cab finally
pulled up, everything in me
shattered. He lifted my bag, placed
it inside gently like it was a piece
of me, and then turned to me. Our
eyes met—and in that glance, we
said it all.
We didn't need I love yous.
 We didn't need promises.
We were two hearts that knew.
That still knows. I reached for his

hand one last time. Held it like it
was the only anchor keeping me
from floating away. And slowly,
painfully… his fingers slipped
from mine. It was like watching the
last scene of a film you never
wanted to end. Like standing still
while the world moves on without
you. I got into the cab, the door
shut between us, and as we pulled
away, I broke. Not because I was
weak, but because I had loved with
my whole soul. I didn't tell him I
love you. Not because I didn't feel
it. But because some loves are too
big for three words. Some loves
live in your bones. In your blood.
In your silences. I loved him when
I had never felt the weight of his
hand in mine. I loved him when he

was miles away, just a dream I
hadn't touched yet. I loved him
without knowing his smell, the
warmth of his skin, the way his
heartbeat sounded when I rested on
his chest. And I loved him like
that. What we have is deeper than
words. It's in the way he wiped the
coffee off my shirt. It's in how he
checked the hot balcony railing
before letting me touch it. It's in
the quiet moments, the laughter,
the stillness. It's in the promise of a
future we haven't built yet—but
already believe in. I left with his
t-shirt. A cute teddy bear and a ring
that still glows on my finger. And a
heart that now beats in a rhythm I
can't unlearn. This isn't over.
 It can't be.

Because I don't just love him.

I am him—in every heartbeat, in every tear, in every hope I still carry.

People say relationships only work if the man loves more. That, unless he's the one chasing, proving, holding everything together, it'll fall apart. But I've never believed that. Not even for a second.

Because love—real love isn't about one person giving more. It's about two people showing up.

Over and over. Even on the hard days. Especially on the hard days.

It's about effort, from both sides. Not grand gestures or perfect moments. But the little things. The quiet sacrifices. The willingness to understand even when it's hard.

The patience to stay when it's
easier to walk away. I don't want a
love where one is constantly
proving, while the other just
receives. I want a love where we
both fight for each other. Where we
both build something with our bare
hands—even if it's messy. Where
he holds my fears like they're his
own. And I hold his dreams like
they're mine. So no, he doesn't
have to love me more.
 He just has to love me enough.
 Enough to try.
Enough to stay.
Enough to believe that what we're
creating is worth it.
 Because I will love with
everything I have. But I need
someone beside me, not behind

me. And if we both give our hearts fully—imperfectly, honestly Then maybe, just maybe, we'll have the kind of love that doesn't just survive… But lasts.

The goodbye we said wasn't a farewell. It was a pause. We have things to fix, bridges to build, hearts to convince. We have to become strong enough not just to love, but to stay. Because real love is brave. And I am ready to fight for mine. If I have to walk through fire, I will. If I have to stand alone, I will. If I have to wait years… I still will. Because this isn't just love. It's my home. And no matter how far I go, my heart will always, always find its way back to him.

Space Between Us

 Coming back to our hometown
after our time together felt both
comforting and cruel. Kabir and I
had returned to the lives we had
pressed pause on—lives filled with
responsibilities, unspoken
expectations, and a clock ticking
somewhere in the background,
reminding us that time was never
truly ours. He buried himself in
work almost immediately. I
watched him slip into his
routine—focused, disciplined,
unwavering. His days stretched
into nights, filled with meetings,
deadlines, and silent tension he
never complained about. He wasn't
avoiding me, not really. He was

just trying to build a future. Our future.

And me?

I filled my hours too—writing, helping around the house, pretending not to notice the way my parents would whisper behind closed doors, pretending not to flinch when another "nice boy" was mentioned during dinner. But no matter how much I kept myself busy, one truth kept returning like a shadow: nothing had changed with my family. Not really. They were still determined to find me a match—someone more suitable, someone from the world they believed I belonged to. Every conversation was dipped in sweet manipulation.

"We're just asking you to meet
him." "At least keep your options
open." "We want what's best for
you." But the unspoken words hurt
more Kabir isn't enough. And still,
the hardest part wasn't fighting
with them. The hardest part was
trying to stay distant from him.
Because how do you maintain
space from the one who feels like
home?
 Every time Kabir brushed past me
with a tired smile, every time his
hand accidentally grazed mine and
lingered for half a second too long,
it got harder to pretend. We had
promised to be careful—for his
sake, for mine—but it felt like
trying to cage a wildfire. At night,
when the world was quiet and no

one was watching, our messages
became softer, sadder.

 "Did you eat?" "You looked tired
today." "I missed you and didn't
know where to put that feeling."
Sometimes, we wouldn't even
speak. We'd just sit in silence on a
call, the comfort of breathing on
the other end becoming the only
peace either of us could find. But I
knew he was slipping away—not
emotionally, but from the space he
used to fill so effortlessly in my
world. He was being careful, too
careful, and I understood why. My
family was everywhere—watching,
judging, deciding. And we… we
were just trying to survive in the
space between love and obligation.

There were moments I wanted to
scream at the walls around me.
To say,
"Why do I have to choose?"
To ask,
"Why is love not enough?"

But all I ever did was smile, nod,
and meet another stranger with
coffee-stained lips and questions
about my dreams—never knowing
they were already shaped like
Kabir. I don't know how long we
can keep living like this.
Loving in quiet corners, hiding in
plain sight.
But for now, we pretend. And in
between pretending, we keep
holding on—barely, but with
everything we have.

Half Love, Whole Ache

We still talk every night.
Nothing's changed—and yet,
everything has. The rhythm of our
conversations is the same: how our
days went,what annoyed us, what
made us laugh, the songs we're
obsessed with. He still tells me to
eat, to take care of myself. Still
reminds me that he's here
whenever I need him. But I've
learned something about love
lately. It's not always about what is
said. It's about what isn't. He tells
me he cares for me. That he has my
back. That he's here. But behind
every word, I hear the hesitation. A
pause. A soft edit to the truth.

"I'll fight for us."

"I won't let anything happen to you."

"I care about you more than you know."

It's like he's building me a safety net made of cotton—soft, warm, comforting—but it never holds my full weight. Because the truth is, Kabir is not sure. Not about me. And I know it.

And yet… His family has started looking for girls. Not just in conversation, but actively. They're sharing pictures, visiting families, and shortlisting profiles. They've decided it's time for Kabir to settle down— with someone from their caste, someone who fits into the life they've imagined for him.

Someone who isn't me. When he told me, his voice was almost apologetic.

"I can't say no to them, Ilahi. They've done everything for me."

And I understood.

That's the part that hurts most—I understood.

He can't say no to his family. They want him to marry within their caste, their world, their comfort zone. And I don't blame them. Not really. That's how they were raised. That's how most people here are raised.

His family isn't just a tradition to him. They're everything. They're the people who raised him, stood by him when he had nothing. And now, he can't stand against them—not for me, not even for himself. But what haunts me is not their expectation—it's his silence. Because every time I talk about the future, he gently redirects the conversation. Every time I ask what he wants—not them, not tradition, not the world—he gives me vague warmth but no certainty. I want to believe him. I want to believe that he'll fight for me. But sometimes, the people who say they'll fight for you are the same ones quietly preparing to surrender. I've always been a fighter. I've challenged my parents. I've questioned traditions. I've stood up to the idea that love doesn't need permission.

But I can't ask him to fight his
only family.
Because that's not love either.
And I don't want to be another
battle in his already war-torn life. I
don't want to be the reason he has
to choose between peace and love.
So instead, we live in this
in-between. We laugh like
nothing's wrong. We text like
always. We smile and send voice
notes and pretend nothing is
burning underneath. We are both
trying to live in the present because
the future feels like a storm we
aren't brave enough to walk into.
But deep inside, I know something
he won't admit: I love him more
than he loves me. He cares. But I
love. He comforts. But I long. He

holds back. But I fall completely.
I'm starting to see it now. Care
isn't the same as certainty. And
comfort isn't the same as
commitment. So I sit with my
feelings quietly. I don't blame him.
I don't demand answers. I just…
wait. For the truth to surface. Or
for my heart to let go, quietly,
without asking for a goodbye.

A Yes, that Broke me

 I don't know what changed.
Maybe nothing did. Maybe I just
got tired of waiting for the moment
when it would. The morning was
soft. Normal. But I wasn't. I had
barely pulled the blanket off my
body when my mother entered the
room, holding her phone like it
carried the future in its palm.
 "They want to come meet you. His
family. He's a good boy. Just talk,
okay?"
I didn't protest. Not today. I went
through the motions—brushed my
hair, wore something elegant, let
them put kajal in my eyes like it
would hide the hollowness behind

them. And I met the boy. He was kind. Gentle. Decent. Everything they wanted. Maybe everything I should have wanted, too. And I said yes. Not because I loved him. Not because I was ready. But because I was done being the only one loving completely. Because I love Kabir with a kind of ache that never fades. The kind that lives in my throat and behind my eyes, waiting to spill. He loves me too—yes, I know he does. But not the way I do.

I love like fire.
Like prayer. Like war.
He loves like shelter.
Like silence.
Like hope that never speaks its name too loudly.

He cares. He listens. He's always
there when I fall. But never once
has he stopped me from walking
away. He says he'll fight for me.
That he has my back. That we're in
this together. And I believe him.
But belief without action feels like
a song on mute—beautiful, but
never loud enough to dance to.
Kabir loves me. I know he does.
But love isn't just words. It's
showing up with your fists
clenched and your heart open. It's
saying, "I choose you"—even
when it's hard, even when you're
scared. And Kabir… He never said
those words out loud. So, I said yes
to someone else.
 Not because I wanted to, but
because I couldn't keep being the

only one choosing us out loud. I couldn't keep writing a love story where he only highlighted the lines I wrote.

 A wedding is being planned. In a month. The mehendi, the music, the meaningless congratulations— they've already begun. I smile in photos, I taste the sweets, I nod when aunties say,
"Finally, Ilahi settled down."
But inside?
 I'm anything but settled. Because I still want him. Because I still love him. Because even now, I lie awake at night, wishing he'd call and say— "No. This isn't how our story ends."
 But I know he won't. Not because he doesn't want me. But because

he doesn't know how to want me
fully.
And I?
I need someone who will love me
as loudly as I love them. So I said
yes. Not to a person. But to peace.
Even if it meant breaking my own
heart.

Things we couldn't say

He Finally Knew** He found out.
Not through me. Through
whispers, maybe. Or a mutual
friend. Or someone's careless story
shared too loudly. But however he
heard it—he did. I remember the
way my phone rang that night. I
stared at his name on the screen
like it was the first time I'd ever
seen it. Like I needed to memorize
the letters before everything
changed. My hands trembled as I
picked up. He didn't say hello.
Just one breath. And then—
"Is it true?"
Three words. No anger. No
judgment. Just a quiet devastation.

I closed my eyes, my chest already
sinking.
 "Yes."
Silence. A long one.
And then— "You said yes?"
 I nodded, even though he couldn't
see me.
"I did."
The air between us shifted. I could
feel his heartbeat in that silence,
even from miles away. Then came
the words I didn't know I'd been
dreading:
 "Why didn't you tell me?"
My throat tightened.
 "Because I didn't know how.
Because I was afraid. Because you
never stopped me."
 I didn't say it to blame him. I said
it because it was the truth. Because

he had all the chances, and he had
always chosen silence. Kindness.
Care. But never action. He didn't
respond right away. And when he
finally did, it wasn't with
questions. It was with honesty.
"I'm not ready, Ilahi."
His voice cracked.
"I love you. You know I do. But
I'm not ready for marriage. Not
yet. I don't have the money. The
stability. I'm still building myself. I
have dreams I haven't touched,
responsibilities I can't ignore, a
family that depends on me."
He wasn't trying to make excuses.
He was trying to breathe.
"And you… you deserve more than
a half-prepared version of me."
That sentence cut deeper than

anything else. Because I didn't
want more. I just wanted him.
"But I love you,"
 I whispered.
"Even now. Even after saying yes.
Even with all this confusion… it's
still you."
My voice broke. I didn't mean to
cry, but I did.
 "Do you think I should tell them?"
I asked.
"My parents? About you? Do I
walk into that room tomorrow and
tell them this isn't what I want?
Or… do I go through with it and
spend the rest of my life wondering
what would've happened if you
had asked me to stay?"

The line was so quiet, I thought he
had hung up. But then I heard him
breathe.
"I don't want to lose you,"
he said.
"But I don't want you to wait for a
future I can't give you right now."
And that was it. No dramatic
confession. No promises. Just
love… incomplete and aching. I sat
on the floor for a long time after
the call ended. The walls around
me were still. My phone screen is
black. The house was silent.
And inside me?
A war.
Because I love him. But I'm
engaged to someone else. Because
I said yes. But I'm still waiting for

him to say Don't. And the most
painful part?
He won't.
Because he loves me too gently.
And I needed someone who would
love me loud enough to stop a
wedding.
 And there I was, all ready…….
 It was after dinner. The plates had
been cleared. My father was
reading the newspaper, and my
mother was scrolling through
images of bridal jewellery on her
phone, showing me screenshots
and smiling like it was the happiest
season of her life. And I? I was
sinking. Every time she said,
"You're going to look so
beautiful," I felt like I was being
dressed for a funeral. Not a person.

But of love. That night, I couldn't carry it anymore. The silence. The pretending. The suffocating pressure of smiles I didn't mean. I stood up, walked to the center of the room, and said quietly "I need to talk to you." They both looked up, instantly alert. I took a deep breath. My heart was pounding in my ears.
"There's something I've been hiding. And I can't anymore."
My mother's smile dropped. My father set the paper down.
"I said yes to this marriage because I thought I had no other choice. Because I thought staying quiet would hurt less than telling you what I feel."
I paused.

"But I love someone else."
The words hung in the air like a
thunderclap. My mother blinked.
My father leaned forward slightly,
not angry — just surprised.
"His name is Kabir," I said, voice
trembling. "We met by chance… or
maybe by fate. I don't know. But I
fell in love with him. Slowly.
Deeply. Honestly."
My mother opened her mouth, but
I kept going. I had to.
"He's not from the same
background. He doesn't come from
money. He isn't ready for marriage
— not yet. He has responsibilities.
A life he's still building. But he
loves me. He cares for me in ways
that no one else ever has."
My voice cracked.

"And I love him… more than I've ever loved anyone. Even after saying yes to someone else. Even after trying to move on. It's still him."
Tears slipped down my face before I could stop them.
 "I didn't tell you earlier because I was scared. Scared you wouldn't understand. Scared you'd think I was being foolish. But the truth is… I'd rather be foolish in love than wise in a life that doesn't belong to me."
 There was silence. Heavy. Unforgiving. My mother's eyes filled with tears. My father looked like he didn't know whether to speak or stay still. So I continued. One last time.

"I'm not asking for permission.
I'm asking for understanding. For
once, I want to choose love, not for
what it gives me, but for what it
makes me feel alive for."
 I wiped my face, trying to gather
myself.
 "I can't marry someone else. Not
when my heart belongs to him."
And then I waited. In that stillness,
I felt every heartbeat, every breath,
every bit of fear I had swallowed
for weeks rise to the surface. But I
didn't regret it. Because finally, I
had said the truth.
Loudly. Bravely. Unapologetically.
 For love.
 For Kabir.
For me.

I Chose You

 I didn't text him this time. I
couldn't. This wasn't something
that could be softened by emojis or
a long-typed message. It had to be
said — with breath, with trembling
voice, with everything my heart
had left to give.
 I called him.
 It rang only once. "Ilahi?"
He always says my name like it's a
question. Like he's checking if I'm
still here. Still his. Tonight, I was.
"I told them."
There was a pause.
Like his body forgot how to
breathe.
"Told who?" he asked softly.

"My parents. About us. About
you. About everything."
 The silence that followed didn't
scare me. Because it was full, not
of fear, but of feeling.
 "You… what?"
"I told them I can't go through
with the wedding,"
 I said.
"That I love someone else. That's
you." I could hear the disbelief in
his breath. "You really did that?"
"Yes." "Ilahi…"
He breathed my name like it was a
prayer.
"I don't know what's going to
happen next,"
 I continued.
 "I don't know if they'll forgive
me. If they'll understand. But I

couldn't lie anymore. Not to them.
Not to myself. Not to you."
 I paused, and then—
 "I chose you, Kabir."
 My voice shook.
"Even if you're not ready. Even if
we don't have it all figured out.
Even if we have to wait. I still
chose you."
He didn't speak. Not right away.
But I didn't fill the silence this
time. I let it stretch, let it settle in
our bones. When he finally spoke,
his voice cracked.
 "Why would you do that for me?"
 I smiled through the tears.
"Because even when you couldn't
say it, I always knew you loved
me. And because… for once in my
life, I didn't want to choose what

was easy. I wanted to choose what
was real."

And then I heard it — the sound of
his tears.

"Ilahi… I don't have anything
figured out. I'm still scared. Still
trying. But I swear, I'll get there.
I'll build that life. I'll give us
everything we deserve."

"We don't need everything," I
whispered. "We just need each
other. And time."

We stayed on the call for hours.
Saying little. Feeling everything.
For the first time in weeks, I slept
with peace instead of pain. Not
because everything was perfect.
But because finally… I wasn't
pretending anymore. I had chosen
love. And love—even scared,

messy, unfinished love—had
chosen me back.

And Now, I Wait**

 It's been a few days. The house is
quieter now—not because the
noise is gone, but because
something inside me has shifted.
My mother doesn't talk about
wedding dates anymore. My father
watches me carefully, like I've
become a stranger he's trying to
understand again. And me? I've
been living in the in-between.
Between fear and faith. Between
the past I walked away from and
the future I still don't fully see.
Some nights I lie awake and ask
myself— Did I do the right thing? I

don't know. I miss the certainty of
being silent. I miss the simplicity
of pretending. But I don't miss the
weight of hiding him. Telling the
truth felt like setting apart of me
free…and binding another in
uncertainty.
 Because Kabir still isn't ready.
Because love didn't magically
solve everything. Because this
choice, as beautiful as it was,
didn't come with guarantees. But I
made it anyway. Not for perfection.
Not for a fairytale. But for peace,
the kind that comes when you
finally stop lying to yourself. I sit
by my window now, more than I
used to.
Watching the sky shift colours.
Watching the world breathe around

me. And sometimes, I whisper into the night—
"I trusted you. Now show me the magic."
 Because somewhere deep down, I still believe the universe listens to hearts like mine — the ones who love, break, and love again without fear. I don't know what tomorrow holds. Maybe my parents will accept us. Maybe they won't. Maybe Kabir will need more time. Maybe he'll surprise me.
 Maybe life will still test us in ways we're not ready for. But what I do know is this: I stood for something real.
 I chose love.
 I chose myself. And now… I wait. For the universe to catch up.

For magic to arrive slowly, softly,
exactly when it's meant to. Just
like Kabir did. Just like I always
believed he would.

Love that stayed quiet

 I thought we had time. We were
finally breathing again. The storm
had passed. I had told my parents.
He had told me he wanted to wait.
His work was going well — that
project with his friend, the one he
used to lose sleep over — it had
finally started taking shape. I saw it
in his voice: the quiet confidence,
the relief. He was slowly becoming
the man he always wanted to be.
And I?
I never felt more sure of us. There
was no rush. No pressure. Just love
— steady, intentional, honest. We
agreed we'd wait. Buy time from
our families. Build ourselves

slowly. And when everything aligned, we'd finally stand side by side, not as a risk… but as a decision. That's what I believed.
 Until he called.
 His voice was soft. Too soft.
"Ilahi… they want me to get engaged."
 I didn't understand at first. Not really. I thought he meant pressure — the usual kind. I thought he'd say he would stall it like before. That he'd hold on. That he'd hold me.
But instead, he said— "I told them about us. I really did. I said everything I could. But they're not ready to accept it… and I don't want to hurt them."

And just like that, I felt something inside me go still.

"So what now?" I asked, though part of me already knew. His voice cracked.

"They've already met the other family. The girl. The rituals are starting. I… I tried, Ilahi. I swear I tried."

He wasn't lying. I could feel it in every word. This wasn't betrayal. This was surrender.

A quiet, helpless surrender from someone who had fought in every way he knew how.

Kabir wasn't selfish. He wasn't cruel. He was just a son — torn between the love that gave him life and the love he found along the way.

And I?
I wasn't angry.
Because even now — with my
heart shattering in slow motion. I
knew he loved me. I knew it in the
way he breathed after saying my
name. In the silence that followed.
In the way he didn't want to let go,
but couldn't find another way to
hold on. He didn't walk away
because he wanted to. He did it
because he couldn't carry everyone
— not his dreams, his parents, his
responsibilities, and me — all at
once.
So I didn't blame him.
I just… broke.
Quietly.
Completely.

Because sometimes love doesn't leave with cruelty — it leaves with care. And that's what hurts the most.

He loved me. But he couldn't choose me.

And I'll spend a lifetime loving him for the boy he was, For the man he tried to become, And for the silence he left me with — full of love, but never loud enough to stay.

One Last Time

 We met quietly. No one knew.
There was no need for witnesses.
No need for explanations. This
moment wasn't for the world. It
was for us — for the love that had
nowhere else to go. I remember the
sound of my heart when I saw him
walk toward me. The way my
breath caught when he looked at
me like I was still his — even
though we both knew I wasn't. We
sat side by side, not too close, not
too far. The kind of distance where
you can still feel someone's
warmth… but not enough to hold
it.
 "You look tired,"

he said softly.
"I haven't been sleeping."
"Me neither."
And that was all it took to bring the
silence down like rain.
"I wanted more time," he
whispered.
"I wanted to become something for
you. Someone worthy."
I shook my head, eyes stinging.
"You were always enough. You
just didn't believe it."
 His fingers brushed mine —
gently, like a goodbye dressed in
affection.
 "I didn't want this to end," he said.
"It's not ending,"
 I replied, voice barely steady.
"It's just… not continuing."

We both laughed — that soft, broken kind of laugh that only comes when there's nothing left to say but everything left to feel. The world outside moved. Lights passed. Cars honked. People laughed somewhere far off. But inside the car, inside this moment, we stopped time. He looked at me with a kind of ache I'll never forget — like he was trying to memorize every inch of my soul in case he forgot how it felt to love me.
 "If there's another life…" he started.
 "Then find me sooner," I whispered. "And fight harder."

Tears slipped down my face before I could stop them. He reached up

to wipe one, but paused halfway —
like even touching me now would
undo the distance we'd worked so
hard to create. So I took his hand
instead. Just for a second. The last
second.
 "Promise me something,"
I said, barely breathing.
 "What?"
 "That you'll remember this. Not as
failure. But as love real, deep, and
honest."
 His voice cracked.
"Ilahi, I'll carry this love with me
for the rest of my life."
And I believed him. Because we
didn't fall out of love. We just fell
out of time. Before I left, I looked
at him one last time. His eyes. My
favorite place in the world.

"Thank you," I whispered.
"For loving me the way you did."
"Thank you," he said back.
"For never asking me to be anyone
else."
I stepped out.
Closed the door. Didn't look back.
Because if I had, I would've
stayed. And love — no matter how
strong — wasn't enough to fight a
life that never made space for us.
But I'll always carry him. In the
songs we used to share. In the
places we never went. In the
version of me that only ever
existed when he was near. And I
know… He'll carry me too. Not as
regret. But as the love that never
left — even when we did.

A Name that Waited

 I didn't see it coming. Just another
slow, golden morning at Fate &
Foam — my café, my sanctuary,
my quiet rebellion. The place
where I stitched myself back
together after years of loving in
silence. After letting go of a boy I
never really stopped carrying. I had
found peace. Not the loud kind.
The kind that sits quietly in your
bones and teaches you to breathe
again. And then the door opened.
And everything stopped. I looked
up — casually, expecting a regular
face, a regular smile — and instead
saw him.
Kabir.

My Kabir.
Time hadn't erased him. It had
deepened him. He looked… older.
Sharper around the edges.
But beautiful, in the way only
someone you once loved with your
whole soul can still look, even after
all the years that swallowed you
both. He didn't see me at first. He
was helping a little girl into a seat.
Her hands were full of crayon
sketches. Her laughter filled the
café like a song I didn't know I'd
been waiting to hear. And then, he
turned.
Our eyes met.
The world blurred.
He froze.
His lips parted.

And in the space between us,
everything came rushing back.
"Ilahi…"
 Just my name. But it carried a
thousand yesterdays. He walked
over slowly, like he wasn't sure I
was real. I wasn't sure either.
 "Is this your place?" he asked
softly, as though even his voice
remembered how to be gentle only
around me.
 "Yeah," I said, trying to smile.
 "I finally built it." He looked
around — the plants, the books, the
corner where I kept poems folded
into teacups.
 "You always said you would," he
said.
"And somehow, I still imagined
you doing it." I tried to hold back

the warmth blooming inside my
chest and the ache that followed
right behind it. Then, the little girl
tugged at his sleeve.
"Papa, can I tell her my name?"
He glanced at her. Then at me.
And my heart already knew.
 "Go ahead," he said softly. She
turned to me, eyes bright.
"My name is Ilahi."
And just like that — The air
vanished from my lungs. Tears
threatened, sudden and fierce. I
looked at him. He looked at me.
And something broke.
Quietly.
Beautifully.
"You named her that…" I
whispered.

He nodded, slowly. His eyes never
left mine.
 "Because I couldn't forget you. I
never did."
My hands trembled, hidden behind
the counter.
 "All these years," he said,
 "I thought I moved on. But I was
only ever moving around you."
 I couldn't speak. I didn't trust my
voice.
He looked at the floor, then back at
me. "It was always you, Ilahi."
His voice cracked.
"Even when I couldn't stay. Even
when I didn't know how to choose.
You were in every breath I took
when I was silent."
 I felt it — the weight of all the
letters I never wrote, the goodbyes

I never said, the part of me that
never stopped hoping fate might
still be listening.
 "I waited," I whispered.
 "Not for you… Just for peace.
And I found it. But God, I still
miss you every day."
He took a breath.
Shaky.
Full of memory.
"I wanted to be the man who
fought the world for you. But I was
scared, Ilahi. Scared of losing
everything. Scared of breaking
what little I had."
I nodded. Because I understood.
More now than I ever did. We
didn't cry. We didn't fall into each
other's arms. We just stood — two
people who had loved in silence

for far too long. He turned to the little girl — my name in her bones — and kissed her forehead. Before he left, he looked at me one last time.

"Even if I never said it loud enough then… I carried you. In every version of me."

And then he walked out.

The door closed.

And I stood still —In the café I built with my own hands, Watching the man I love walk away one last time, With the only echo of us left holding his hand.

 A little girl named Ilahi.

And somehow, that was enough.

It was Forever

 I never saw him again after that
day. He walked out of Fate &
Foam with a child holding his
hand, and left behind a silence that
didn't hurt. Not this time. Because
for the first time in years, I didn't
feel like something had ended. I
felt like something had finally…
settled. All this time, I thought love
had to arrive with forever. That it
had to end with a name change,
with vows, with a lifetime spent
side by side. But that day, when he
looked at me with a heart full of
regret and a child full of memory, I
understood something I had never
been brave enough to admit:

Sometimes, the truest kind of love is the one that lets go. Love isn't always about staying. It's about wishing someone well even as they walk into a life that doesn't have you in it. It's about carrying someone softly in the corners of your soul, even when your hands aren't allowed to hold them anymore. It's not about being chosen. It's about having felt that kind of love at all. And I did. I loved him. I still do. And I probably always will. But that love no longer needs a place at the table. It doesn't ask questions. It doesn't ache for answers. It just exists — quietly. Like music in another room. Like a name written in the first page of an old journal

— worn, but never erased. I'll never be his. And he'll never be mine. But somewhere in the quiet between two lifetimes, we'll always belong to each other. Not in the way we dreamed. But in the way we survived each other. I still smile when I think of him. Sometimes when I make coffee. Sometimes, when I water the flowers by the window. Sometimes, when a stranger laughs the way he used to. And I know —
You don't have to be in someone's life to love them. You just have to let them live freely in your heart. That's the kind of love I carry now.
Not heavy.
Not loud.
Just mine. Forever.

Epilogue

For the Ones Who Loved Quietly
If you're reading this, I hope you
know: Not every love story is
meant to be lived out loud. Some
love stories don't end in marriage.
They don't end in promises or
photos or shared last names. Some
love stories are meant to be felt,
not finished. I loved once. So
deeply, it changed me. And though
life didn't let that love stay, it never
truly left. It lives in the way I smile
when no one's looking. In the café
I built with my own hands. In the
strength I found after choosing
myself. In the silence I learned to
keep sacred. He was never mine in

the way the world defines
"forever." But in the quietest parts
of my soul — he always will be.
And maybe… that's enough.
Because loving someone doesn't
mean holding them. It means
letting them be free — and still
choosing to carry them gently
within you. This is not a story of
loss. It's a story of becoming. Of
surviving love, and still choosing
to believe in it. So if you're still
holding on to a name you haven't
spoken in years — If you're still
loving someone from a distance —
If you're still hoping that time will
understand what the world never
did — Just know this:
 You are not alone. And some
love… They don't die.

They just learn how to live
differently. – Charu

About The Author

Charu Maggo is an emerging author with a deep passion for storytelling, exploring the complexities of human emotions, love, and fate. Born with a vivid imagination and a natural gift for writing, Charu has always been captivated by how life's twists and turns lead people to unexpected destinies. Her debut novel, Between Life and Fate, is a testament to her ability to craft compelling, heartfelt narratives that capture the essence of love and the transformative power of fate. Charu's writing reflects her deep understanding of human relationships and her ability to intertwine the nuances of culture, family, and personal struggles. Charu takes readers on a poignant, emotional journey through the life of Ilahi, a young woman torn between love and her family's expectations. The book resonates with readers who have ever had to fight for love or follow their hearts despite life's obstacles. When she's not writing, Charu enjoys reading, exploring new cultures, and delving into the mysteries of the universe. Her experiences and her belief in the power of fate and love fuel her creativity, and she hopes her stories inspire others to never give up on what truly matters. With a pen that can tug at the

heartstrings and create
unforgettable moments, Charu
Maggo is an author whose future
works will undoubtedly leave a
lasting impact on readers
everywhere.